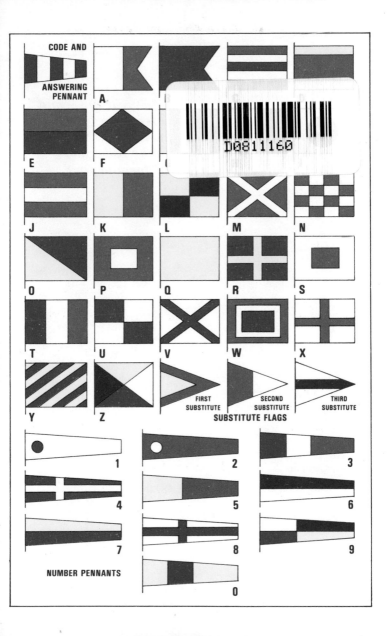

Sending secret messages can be great fun – and very useful at times! As you read this book, you will probably want to make your own code book. Try making up some codes and ciphers, and keep a record of them in your book.

First edition

Codes and Ciphers

by J C HAWTIN

designed and illustrated
by HURLSTON DESIGN LTD

Ladybird Books Loughborough

CODES AND CIPHERS

Codes and ciphers (sigh-fers) are both used to turn plain messages or *plaintexts* into secret messages or *cryptograms* (krip-toe-grams). The word 'cryptogram' comes from the Greek words *kryptos* meaning 'secret', and *graphein* meaning 'to write'.

A code (from the Latin *codex* meaning 'book') may be made up of code words, code numbers or code signs to stand in place of whole plaintext words. Part of a code is shown on the next page.

A cipher (from the Arabic *cifr* meaning 'empty') does not work quite like a code. A cipher takes the single letters which made up the plaintext words and mixes up (or hides) these letters, so that the words they make cannot be understood. When a cipher mixes up plaintext letters it is *transposing*, but if it uses other letters, numbers or signs to hide the plaintext then it is *substituting*.

When plaintexts are turned into cryptograms by code, we say that the plaintexts have been *encoded*. Plaintexts which are turned into cryptograms by cipher have been *enciphered*.

Lastly, if we wish to understand cryptograms made from codes, we must *decode* them to get their plaintext meaning. Cryptograms made from ciphers must be *deciphered* to find their plaintext meanings.

ENCODING

Part of a code is shown below. The plaintext words can be encoded by their numbers.

Plaintext	Code	Plaintext	Code	Plaintext	Code
Stay away	68	Today	72	Unless	76
Stay hidden	69	Tomorrow	73	Until	77
Stay inside	70	Tonight	74	Upon	79
Stay silent	71	Under	75	Vanish	80

Example of Encoding

Plaintext	Stay hidden	until	tomorrow
Cryptograms	69	77	73

ENCIPHERING

We can encipher a message by mixing up the plaintext letters (transposing) or by using other letters, numbers or signs to stand for the plaintext letters (substituting).

Examples of enciphering

Plaintext   **BAD DOG**

Cryptograms   1 **A B D   D G O**   by transposing letters

2 **02 01 04   04 15 07**   by substituting numbers for letters

3 ⊔ ⊔ ⊐   ⊐•⊓   by substituting signs for letters

DECODING AND DECIPHERING

To decode and decipher the cryptograms quickly, we need first of all to know how the codes and ciphers have been made up. Then, using this information, we can work backwards to the plaintext.

Now see if you can sort out these letters to make the names of famous cities:

LNNODO   SPAIR   KOOTY   MERO   BNOSIL
LERNIB   TOATWA   COOWSM   IRAOC   SOOL

CODES AND CIPHERS
IN BIBLICAL TIMES

The priests and scribes in ancient India and Egypt knew how to make cryptograms. In the sixth century BC, the Israelites also enciphered words in their writings. For example in the Holy Bible, the Book of Jeremiah, Chapter 25 verse 26, has the word *Sheshach* used in place of the word Babel. Babel (or Babylon) was a great kingdom and enemy of the Israelites.

Later, a code sign was used by followers of Jesus Christ during the times after His crucifixion. Then, the Romans were taking Christians who would not give up their faith and were putting them into prison or killing them.

These early Christians saw that they needed to help each other in times of danger. This meant that they also needed to recognise each other without giving themselves away to their enemies. So the Christians made themselves a code sign which *they* could understand, but their enemies could not.

Their sign was a fish — and this is why. In those times Greek was widely spoken, and in Greek *Iesous Christos Theou Uios Soter* means 'Jesus Christ Son of God, Saviour'. Now if the leading letters of these Greek words are taken — I, Ch, Th, U, S — they spell ICHTHUS, which is Greek for 'fish'. So followers of Jesus could draw the fish sign, or say the word ICHTHUS, to show secretly that they were Christians and would help each other.

THE ANCIENT
SPARTAN SKYTALE

By the fourth century BC, the army commanders of the ancient Spartans could send cryptograms among themselves which their enemies could not understand. To do this they used a simple wooden cylinder called a *skytale* (ski-ta-li).

A long strip of skin or parchment was wound closely around the skytale, and the plaintext message was written along the length of the strip. The strip was then unwound to make the plaintext words break up into a cryptogram. The cryptogram could only be understood by other Spartan commanders who had skytales of just the same shape as the one used in writing the messages. When such messages were delivered they were rewound on these other skytales so that letters and words would take shape again and could be read.

Send your own message the Spartan way. Take a cardboard tube (a sweet tube will do). Next, cut a strip of paper 1 cm wide and wind this around the tube, overlapping slightly. The overlap keeps the strip in place as you write on it.

Write your plaintext message across the tube and fill in any spaces with *nulls* (letters having no meaning). When the message is unwound, it will be just a strip of paper filled with meaningless letters. Only when a friend winds the strip around a similar tube will the message be revealed.

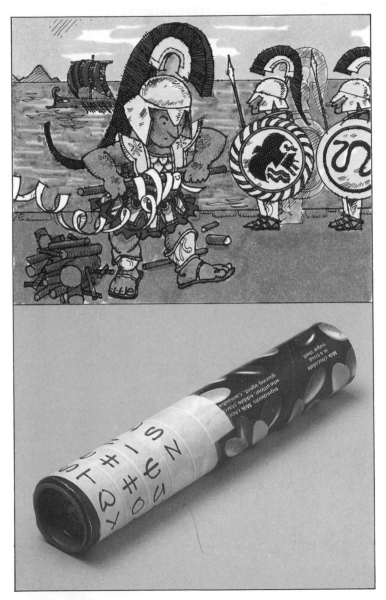

POLYBIUS' CIPHER

The Romans found it very useful to be able to send secret messages to friends and allies, and during Roman times new ciphers came into being. Polybius (second century BC) was a Greek who served the Romans, and it was he who devised a way to replace plaintext with numbers. He did this by drawing a grid of 25 squares, 5 by 5. He then wrote the alphabet in these 25 squares. Notice that when we use the English alphabet X and Y are squeezed into one square. Then he numbered the rows and columns. Each letter of your message can be enciphered by writing firstly the number of the row, and then the number of the column in which the letter lies. So in the grid below E becomes 15, and O becomes 35.

COLUMNS

	1	2	3	4	5
1	A	B	C	D	E
2	F	G	H	I	J
3	K	L	M	N	O
4	P	Q	R	S	T
5	U	V	W	XY	Z

ROWS

Using Polybius' square, see if you can encipher the following:

**LEMON LIME ORANGE APPLE CHERRY
GRAPEFRUIT TANGERINE GRAPE PLUM DATE**

Also try to decipher these words:

12	11	34	11	34	11		41	15	11	13	23
44	32	35	15		41	15	11	43
43	11	44	41	12	15	43	43	54
14	11	33	44	35	34		33	11	34	22	35
11	41	43	24	13	35	45
41	24	34	15	11	41	41	32	15
13	51	43	43	11	34	45

CAESAR'S ALPHABET

Later, it is said, Julius Caesar (100 BC-44 BC) sent cryptograms to his friends by using a cipher alphabet which, to this day, is called Caesar's alphabet. The normal plaintext was written out and underneath was placed his cipher alphabet beginning with D. So instead of using the top letters to make his words, Caesar used the letters below, so that BAD DOG for example would become EDG GRJ.

A	B	C	D	E	F	G	H	I	J	K	L	M
D	E	F	G	H	I	J	K	L	M	N	O	P

N	O	P	Q	R	S	T	U	V	W	X	Y	Z
Q	R	S	T	U	V	W	X	Y	Z	A	B	C

Of course your own cipher alphabet does not have to start with D — you could use any letter. In order to change your cipher alphabet, a cipher slide can easily be made like the one shown on page 39. Then just choose a letter to start your cipher alphabet, slide that letter below A in the plaintext alphabet, and you can easily encipher a message by reading downwards. If your friends have similar slides, and use the same cipher alphabets as you do, they can then decipher your message by reading upwards.

Using your slide, see if you can encipher these words into Caesar's D cipher:

SEASONS SPRING SUMMER AUTUMN WINTER CHRISTMAS

Now try to decipher these words, once again using Caesar's D cipher:

MDQXDUB OHQW GHFHPEHU HDVWHU MXQH IHEUXDUB

EARLY CODES IN CHINA

Codes, like ciphers, were also used in early times to send important messages secretly or briefly. One such early code was being used by the Chinese in the eleventh century AD. Like the early Spartans in Greece, the Chinese army commanders had to be able to send and receive messages which their enemies could not read. To do this, the Chinese used a set of code signs.

Thirty or forty of the signs which are used in Chinese writings were picked out, and each sign was given a plaintext meaning. For example, the sign for 'cloud' 云 could mean 'we are short of food – please send more.' The sign for 'rain' 雨 could mean 'we need more spears and shields', and the sign for 'snow' 雪 could mean 'we have won a great battle.'

The Army Commander would write down the signs that he needed to make up his message. His men would decode the signs (from a code book), and could then act upon the news or orders written in the coded message.

Below are the Chinese signs for numbers 1 to 12. Make up your own code by giving each sign a plaintext meaning. For example, 1 一 could mean 'Meet after school', 2 二 could mean 'A bike ride tomorrow', and so on.

1 一	4 四	7 七	10 十
2 二	5 五	8 八	11 十一
3 三	6 六	9 九	12 十二

When you have decided on your code, you and a friend could then enter this code in your code and cipher books.

DIAGRAM CIPHERS

One kind of cipher turns plaintext letters into secret signs. This is called a *diagram* cipher. The diagram cipher shown below is called a *pig-pen* cipher. It was widely used in the sixteenth century by the Freemasons, a secret society that was begun by King Solomon's stonemasons in the tenth century BC. The cipher is easy to set up and just as easy to use. Letters A to I are written inside an open grid. Letters J to M are placed between two crossed lines (diagonals). Next, letters N to V are written inside another grid but dots are put below each letter (the dots are the 'pigs', the lines make the 'pens'). Lastly, letters W to Z are placed between diagonals again but with dots between letters and lines.

A	B	C	J	N̤	O̤	P̤	W
D	E	F	K L	Q̤	R̤	S̤	X · · Y
G	H	I	M	T̤	Ṳ	V̤	Z

Making cryptograms is quite easy. You just have to draw the shapes made by lines and dots round the plaintext letters instead of writing the letters themselves – like this:

M E E T   Y O U   A T   M I D N I G H T

16

You can make your own pig-pen cipher by putting the alphabet into the grids and diagonals in a different order. For example, you could put the letters in reverse order. Your own pig-pen cipher could then be put into your code and cipher book. Using the pig-pen opposite, try to encipher the names of these countries:

BRITAIN GERMANY DENMARK SWITZERLAND PORTUGAL

What are these words?

⊏⊡⊐⊍⊏⊏⊏⊐⊏ ⊼⊡⊳⊏⊏⊍ ⊏⊡⊐⊐⊡

⊏⊽⊡⊐⊐⊡ ⊏⊿⊡⊏⊓⊍⊏⊏⊏⊏⊐⊐⊏

GRILLE CIPHER

The Italian Jerome Cardano (1501-1576) is said to have first made the *grille cipher* in order to send secret messages. The grille is a piece of paper with holes cut in it. An ordinary message can then be sent and by placing the grille over that message the words of the secret message are revealed.

This is how to make a simple grille cipher so that you can send a secret message:

1 Write an innocent letter containing the words of your secret message, in the correct order.
2 Place a piece of tracing paper over your letter and draw rectangles around your secret words.
3 Cut out the rectangles.
4 Make a similar grille to give to your friend, so that he or she will be able to read your secret message, by placing the grille over your letter. The words of your message will appear inside the 'windows' of the grille.

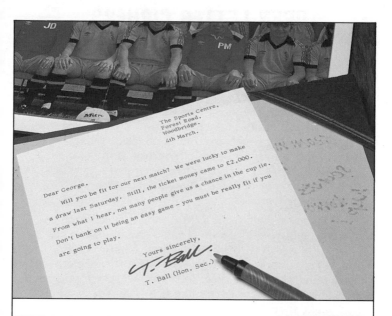

The Sports Centre,
Forest Road,
Woodbridge,
4th March.

Dear George,

Will you be fit for our next match? We were lucky to make a draw last Saturday. Still, the ticket money came to £2,000.

From what I hear, not many people give us a chance in the cup tie. Don't bank on it being an easy game – you must be really fit if you are going to play.

Yours sincerely,

T. Ball (Hon. Sec.)

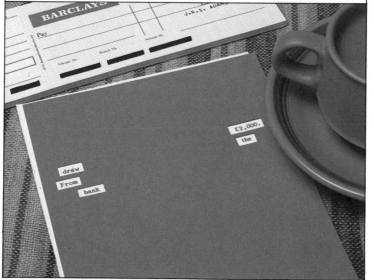

OPEN LETTER CIPHERS

Another clever way of sending cryptograms is to use an *Open Letter Cipher*. Many important messages have been sent like this in the past. Anyone can easily make this kind of cipher. The idea is to hide your secret message inside what looks like a normal open letter. How is the cipher set up? One way is to write an open letter in which the capitals not only start the sentences but also make your secret message.

Maybe this will need a little care at first. Each sentence in your open letter must make sense. Only use easy words to begin with. Neat handwriting is also very important. Make your open letters easy to read and also make them look normal. Once you have written a few letters like this, you will be able to make them up more quickly.

Now have a close look at the open letter on the next page. Do you see there how the cryptogram is made by the 10 capital letters which also start the sentences?

All sentences in your open letters must go well together so that no one can guess that they hide a cryptogram. You can see this done on the next page and you can also find a cryptogram on *this page* if you write down the capital letters which start the sentences here.

25 Royal Road
York
1st June

Dear James,

Are you feeling better now? Mother says you must come to visit us. I am looking forward to seeing you again. Never mind about the buses and train times, father will fetch you in our car. Let us know when he can call for you. Our car is a nice one. Ninety miles an hour is its top speed. Do you like fast cars? Once father is on the motorway he will soon have you here. Next week would be a good time to come.

Love,

Anne.

21

THE ZIGZAG CIPHER

Jumbling (or *transposing*) the letters which make up the words is one way of setting up a cipher, and a very easy way of transposing letters in short messages is to use *zigzag* writing.

This kind of writing is like normal writing because it is written from left to right in lines. However, unlike normal writing, it does *not* run in straight lines. Instead, each letter is written in turn, above and below a line, making the message take on a zigzag shape.

Normal writing **WHEN DOES THE BOAT LEAVE**

Zigzag writing **W E DE TE OT EV**

                       H N O S H B A L A E

All we have to do to make a cryptogram from the zigzag writing is to write down all of the letters *above* the line: W E D E T E O T E V. Then follow with the letters *below* the line: H N O S H B A L A E. So the full cryptogram would be WEDETEOTEV—HNOSHBALAE.

When your friends get such messages they must write the letters before the hyphen above a line, and the letters after the hyphen below the same line, and your cryptogram will be solved.

22

Practise the zigzag code by enciphering these messages:

CAN YOU READ THIS
WHEN IS YOUR BIRTHDAY   HOW OLD ARE YOU

Can you decipher these zigzag messages?

WAIYUNM—HTSORAE
HWALRYU—OTLAEO   HWUHOOWIH—OMCDYUEG

THE BOOK CODE

Did you know that you can use almost any book to set up a code? This is called a *Book code*, and it changes plaintext messages into cryptograms made up of numbers.

Suppose you wish to encode the message **NEED FOOD** by using *this Ladybird book* as your code book. What you must do is to take each plaintext word and find it in this book. As you find each word, write down:

(a) The number of the page, then a full stop.

(b) The number of the line on which the word lies, then a full stop. Count lines from top to bottom. Page headings do not count as lines.

(c) The position of the word along the line (first, second, third...). then a full stop.

The full stops will keep the numbers from mixing up.

Your plaintext **NEED FOOD** can be encoded like this: **NEED** becomes **48.6.4** because it is found on page **48** on line **6** and it is the fourth word on that line.

FOOD becomes **14.13.1** because it is found on page **14** on line **13** and it is the first word on that line.

The full cryptogram will be **48.6.4 14.13.1**.

To decode such cryptograms, you need to know which book has been used as the code book. Remember that the figures in turn tell you a page number, a line number and a place number.

You can make encoded messages very quickly in this way — try using a dictionary for your code book, and make up a book code.

TRANSPOSING IN ROWS AND COLUMNS

Another way to transpose letters is by using rows going across and columns going down. In this method the letters are written − in oblongs or squares called *arrays* − in one order, and are then rewritten in another order.

The example below has a plaintext message: **PLANE LEAVING TODAY.** This message has 17 letters and will not fit into an oblong shape, so we add Z as a null to give us 18 letters. Now we can write the 18 letters into an array containing 3 rows of 6 columns:

> **P L A N E L**
> **E A V I N G**
> **T O D A Y Z**

We can now encipher the plaintext by writing the columns in groups of three: **PET LAO AVD NIA ENY LGZ.** When you send this message, your friend just has to write the groups down in columns, then by reading the rows the message is revealed.

Here is another example. Suppose we want to send the message: **MEET YOU BY THE LARGE OAK.** These 20 letters can be arranged into an array of 4 rows of 5 columns:

> **M E E T Y**
> **O U B Y T**
> **H E L A R**
> **G E O A K**

which we can encipher as

MOHG EUEE EBLO TYAA YTRK

Now see if you can encipher these messages by arranging them in 4 × 4 arrays:

WHEN CAN YOU TRAVEL

WRITE OUT YOUR PLAN

And try to decipher these messages which have also been arranged in 4 × 4 arrays:

KIOO ENSU ECEC PLTH

SSSI HATG IIOH PLNT

Start by writing the letters in columns, *eg*

K
I
O
O

27

KEY NUMBER CIPHERS

Cryptograms from rows and columns are made even more secret if you move the rows and columns about before you make your cryptograms. To show how this is done, here is an example. **SEND HELP BEFORE NEXT WEEKEND** is the message.

To start with, write the 25 plaintext letters in a square having 5 rows of 5 letters, then number each column at the top:

1	2	3	4	5
S	E	N	D	H
E	L	P	B	E
F	O	R	E	N
E	X	T	W	E
E	K	E	N	D

Now move the columns about, but keeping the same number above the same columns:

5	2	4	1	3
H	E	D	S	N
E	L	B	E	P
N	O	E	F	R
E	X	W	E	T
D	K	N	E	E

Lastly, write the rows in groups of 5. Your secret message will read **HEDSN ELBEP NOEFR EXWET DKNEE**, with the key number **5 2 4 1 3**.

To decipher such a message, your friend needs to know the key number and also how the original message was arranged: in this case 52413 and a 5 × 5 array. Then it is a simple task of working backwards. Write out the key number, and under the key number write the groups of letters in rows across. Now re-arrange the numbers and letters under them into a 12345 order — and the message can be read.

Encipher these messages writing them in a 5 × 5 array, and re-arranging the columns into a 54321 order:

TELEPHONE ME TOMORROW AT NOON

HIDE THE PAPERS IN A SAFE PLACE

These messages have been enciphered in a key number cipher. The key number is 23541, and the messages were written in a 5 × 5 array:

ECPID ERHTH SCYRI TORGP MNWOA

EAEVL ALAFH HORUN FTREA UNHCL

What are the messages?

SUPER-ENCIPHERMENT AND ENCICODE

To make a secret message, the plaintext is either encoded or enciphered into a cryptogram. That cryptogram can be made even more secret if you treat it as a new plaintext and then encode or encipher it again to make a second cryptogram. In other words, the first plaintext will be made into a cryptogram twice over.

When both first and second cryptogram are made from different ciphers, this method is called **super-encipherment** (Latin 'super' meaning above, on top of). Sometimes the first cryptogram is made from code and then a cipher is used on it to give the second cryptogram.

This is called **enciphered code** (or 'encicode' for short).

Some examples of super-encipherment and encicode are shown below.

Super-encipherment Both cryptograms from ciphers

Plaintext **BAD DOG**

1st cryptogram **EDG GRJ** (from Caesar's D cipher alphabet on page 12)

The pig-pen cipher can now be used to encipher the first cryptogram which is our new plaintext.

New plaintext **EDG GRJ**

2nd cryptogram □ ⊐ ⌐ ⌐⊡ ∨ (from the pig-pen cipher)

Encicode 1st cryptogram from code, 2nd cryptogram from cipher.

Plaintext   **NEED FOOD**

1st cryptogram   **48.6.4 14.13.1**   (encoded by this book's own code)

We now use the cipher below to encipher the coded figures.

$$Z=0 \quad Y=1 \quad X=2 \quad W=3 \quad V=4 \quad U=5$$
$$T=6 \quad S=7 \quad R=8 \quad Q=9$$

New plaintext   **48. 6. 4 14.13.1**

2nd cryptogram   **VR.T.V YV.YW.Y**

To decode or decipher such cryptograms as those above, you need to know which codes and ciphers have been used, and in which order.

Now try to decipher these messages, using first the pig-pen and then Caesar's D cipher:

✓><⌐ <⌐ ⊐ >⊐⊓⊓ ⌐⊓◻◻⊔⊓⌐
⊓<⊓ ⊔◻> ∨⊓∨ ✓>⊓ ⊐◻⌐∧⊓⊓

Also see if you can decode these messages using the letter and number cipher above and then this book's code:

YZ.YY.Q.XV.Y.X.R.V.Y.XR.V.V.

VT.X.Y.R.R.Y.XV.X.S.WR.X.W.WZ.YV.S.

31

KEYWORD CIPHERS

Another Italian, Giambattista della Porta (c. 1538-1615), first used **keyword ciphers** by making a letter table (opposite). The alphabet letters are paired and written as capitals in a column. To their right are small letter alphabets in two lines. The alphabet next to AB is normal but the one next to CD has Z written between m and n, and the one next to EF has y z written between m and n. This goes on to give thirteen different cipher alphabets.

Keywords, showing which cipher alphabets must be used, are made from the capitals.

Let us encipher '**need help**', using the keyword **PIN** (pick keywords with all letters different).

First write the plaintext   **n e e d   h e l p**

Then write the keyword
repeating as necessary   **P I N P   I N P I**

To encipher **n**, the keyword shows that the alphabet opposite **P** must be used. Find **n** in that alphabet, and write down its partner (**h**). To encipher **e**, the keyword shows that the alphabet opposite **I** is used. Find **e** there and write down its partner (**n**). Carry on to get **h n y w q y r g**.

To decipher you must know the keyword and then work backwards.

First the cryptogram: **h n y w q y r g**

Then the keyword: **P I N P I N P I**

To decipher **h** you must use the alphabet opposite **P**. Write down the partner of **h** in that alphabet (**n**). To decipher **n**, use the alphabet opposite **I**. Write down the partner of **n** there (**e**). Carry on for the full plaintext.

PORTA'S TABLE

	a	b	c	d	e	f	g	h	i	j	k	l	m
A B	n	o	p	q	r	s	t	u	v	w	x	y	z
C D	z	n	o	p	q	r	s	t	u	v	w	x	y
E F	y	z	n	o	p	q	r	s	t	u	v	w	x
G H	x	y	z	n	o	p	q	r	s	t	u	v	w
I J	w	x	y	z	n	o	p	q	r	s	t	u	v
K L	v	w	x	y	z	n	o	p	q	r	s	t	u
M N	u	v	w	x	y	z	n	o	p	q	r	s	t
O P	t	u	v	w	x	y	z	n	o	p	q	r	s
Q R	s	t	u	v	w	x	y	z	n	o	p	q	r
S T	r	s	t	u	v	w	x	y	z	n	o	p	q
U V	q	r	s	t	u	v	w	x	y	z	n	o	p
W X	p	q	r	s	t	u	v	w	x	y	z	n	o
Y Z	o	p	q	r	s	t	u	v	w	x	y	z	n

Can you encipher these messages, using Porta's Table?

Keyword: **WATER**

THE SUNSET IS IN THE WEST.
THE FULL MOON IS BRIGHT.

Also try to decipher these messages:

Keyword: **QUICK**

vqiw xqllpk tbrbo mqrb kbliyk.
xbfgl skz gfjg ycuw ye kqidnf.

The Frenchman Blaise de Vigénère (born 1523) took keyword ciphers further by writing a table of 26 cipher alphabets (opposite). Plaintext alphabets in capitals run along the top, bottom and down the left-hand side. The left-hand side capitals start their own cipher alphabets running to their right. These capitals are also used for the keywords.

Use the keyword **BLUE** and the table to encipher **SEND GOLD COINS.**

First the plaintext   **S E N D G O L D C O I N S**

Then the keyword
repeated as necessary   **B L U E B L U E B L U E B**

To encipher **S**, the keyword tells you to use the **B** cipher alphabet, so find **B** on the left-hand side and trace its alphabet (**b, c, d . . .**) across the page until you are under **S** at the top. Write the letter there (**t**). To encipher **E**, you must use the **L** cipher alphabet, so find **L** on the left. Trace its alphabet until you are under **E** at the top. Write the letter there (**p**). Your full cryptogram will be **tphh hzfh dzcrt**. To decipher, you must know the keyword and work backwards.

First the cryptogram: **t p h h h z f h d z c r t**

Then the keyword: **B L U E B L U E B L U E B**

To decipher **t**, the keyword shows you must use the **B** alphabet, so find **t** in that alphabet and write the CAPITAL letter which is straight above it (**S**). To decipher **p**, use the **L** alphabet. Find **p** in that alphabet and write down the CAPITAL letter above it (**E**). Carry on like this for the full plaintext.

THE VIGÉNÈRE TABLE

```
  A B C D E F G H I J K L M N O P Q R S T U V W X Y Z
A a b c d e f g h i j k l m n o p q r s t u v w x y z
B b c d e f g h i j k l m n o p q r s t u v w x y z a
C c d e f g h i j k l m n o p q r s t u v w x y z a b
D d e f g h i j k l m n o p q r s t u v w x y z a b c
E e f g h i j k l m n o p q r s t u v w x y z a b c d
F f g h i j k l m n o p q r s t u v w x y z a b c d e
G g h i j k l m n o p q r s t u v w x y z a b c d e f
H h i j k l m n o p q r s t u v w x y z a b c d e f g
I i j k l m n o p q r s t u v w x y z a b c d e f g h
J j k l m n o p q r s t u v w x y z a b c d e f g h i
K k l m n o p q r s t u v w x y z a b c d e f g h i j
L l m n o p q r s t u v w x y z a b c d e f g h i j k
M m n o p q r s t u v w x y z a b c d e f g h i j k l
N n o p q r s t u v w x y z a b c d e f g h i j k l m
O o p q r s t u v w x y z a b c d e f g h i j k l m n
P p q r s t u v w x y z a b c d e f g h i j k l m n o
Q q r s t u v w x y z a b c d e f g h i j k l m n o p
R r s t u v w x y z a b c d e f g h i j k l m n o p q
S s t u v w x y z a b c d e f g h i j k l m n o p q r
T t u v w x y z a b c d e f g h i j k l m n o p q r s
U u v w x y z a b c d e f g h i j k l m n o p q r s t
V v w x y z a b c d e f g h i j k l m n o p q r s t u
W w x y z a b c d e f g h i j k l m n o p q r s t u v
X x y z a b c d e f g h i j k l m n o p q r s t u v w
Y y z a b c d e f g h i j k l m n o p q r s t u v w x
Z z a b c d e f g h i j k l m n o p q r s t u v w x y
  A B C D E F G H I J K L M N O P Q R S T U V W X Y Z
```

Practise using the Vigénère Table to encipher these messages:

Keyword: **YOUNG**

A LION ROARS   **SNAKES HISS**
SHEEP BLEAT   **WOLVES HOWL**

Also try to decipher these:

Keyword: **PRIZE**

wvvr gptski   pe wvp wfwsw
slkjw flibo   pe irw qiixw

CIPHER DISCS

The Italian Leon Battista Alberti (1404-1472) first used cipher discs to give himself 26 cipher alphabets for writing cryptograms. Make your own discs (as shown opposite) and use them to encipher **IT IS AT HOME**, using the keyword **WORLD**.

Plaintext	I T	I S	A T	H O M E
Keyword	W O	R L	D W	O R L D

The keyword shows that you must encipher **I** by using a **W** cipher alphabet. To make this, turn the cipher disc until **W** is under plaintext **A** on the larger disc. Find **I** on this disc and write down the letter lying under it on your cipher disc (**E**). To encipher **E**, you must use an **O** cipher alphabet. Turn the cipher disc until its **O** is under plaintext **A**. Find **T** on the larger disc and write the letter lying under it on the cipher disc (**H**). Your cryptogram will be **E H Z D D P V F X H**.

To decipher, you must know the keyword and work backwards.

First the cryptogram:	E H Z D D	P V F X H
Then the keyword:	W O R L D	W O R L D

To decipher **E**, you need the **W** cipher alphabet, so turn the cipher disc until its **W** is under plaintext **A**. Find **E** on the cipher disc and write the letter lying above it on the larger disc (**I**). To decipher **H**, use the **O** cipher alphabet. Turn the cipher disc until its **O** is under plaintext **A**. Find **H** on the cipher disc and write the letter lying above it on the larger plaintext disc (**T**). Carry on for the full plaintext.

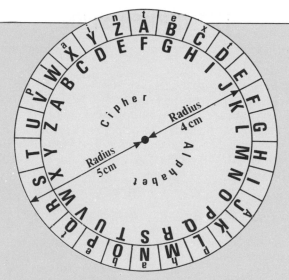

To make a cipher disc:

1 Cut two card discs, one with a 4 cm radius, the other with a 5 cm radius.
2 Divide the discs into 26 equal sectors (these sectors are about 14° each), and write the alphabet around the edges of the two discs.
3 Label the large disc plaintext, and the small disc cipher alphabet.
4 Fasten the discs together at their centre with a paper fastener, so that the small disc moves over the large one.

Now use your cipher disc to encipher these messages:

Keyword: **BOXES**

SEND ME CASH   **GIVE HIM HELP**

HIDE IT AWAY

And decipher these:

Keyword: **DREAM**

SRVK FKV GAD   **PROE UW NSRW**

FRR YAX JIE UW   **OZWTQQ KS HQU**

THE CIPHER SLIDE

The *St Cyr cipher slide* was widely used by the French army in the last century. Make your own slide from card (as shown opposite). Like the cipher discs, the slide can help you to set up 26 cipher alphabets in a short time. Use your slide to encipher **BUY A NEW CAR**, taking the keyword **MONEY**.

Plaintext	**B U Y**	**A**	**N E W**	**C A R**
Keyword	**M O N**	**E**	**Y M O**	**N E Y**

Remember the keyword always shows which cipher alphabets to use, so to encipher **B** we need a **M** cipher alphabet. To set this up, slide the cipher strip until **M** comes under plaintext **A** (on the top). Write down the letter on the strip which is under plaintext **B** (N). To encipher **U**, you need the **O** cipher alphabet, so slide the strip until its **O** is under plaintext **A**. Write down the letter on the strip which is under **U** (I). The full cryptogram is **NILE L QKPEP.**

To decipher, work backwards:

First the cryptogram:	**N I L**	**E**	**L Q K**	**P E P**
Then the keyword:	**M O N**	**E**	**Y M O**	**N E Y**

To decipher **N**, use the **M** cipher alphabet. Slide the strip until **M** is under plaintext **A**. Find **N** on the strip and write the plaintext letter above it (**B**). To decipher **I**, use the **O** cipher alphabet. Slide the strip until **O** lies under plaintext **A**. Find **I** on the strip and write down the plaintext letter above it (**U**). Carry on for the full plaintext.

THE CIPHER SLIDE

Letters are in spaces of 5 millimetres

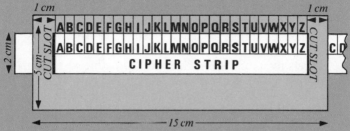

CIPHER STRIP

Letter spaces are 5 millimetres

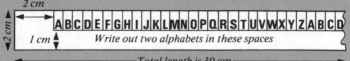

Write out two alphabets in these spaces

Total length is 30 cm

Push the cipher strip through the slots as in the top diagram

Practise using your slide by enciphering and deciphering these messages. Remember to use the keywords.

Encipher   Keyword: **KINGS**

SEND REPORTS TO ME
WRITE YOUR REPORTS IN CIPHER

Decipher   Keyword: **BARON**

NUJH UFAI TEPM PCH UOUOL
VSV O XFYNCEE CZDUFR

CIPHER WHEELS

Thomas Jefferson (1743-1826), a President of the USA, first had the idea of using cipher wheels – that is a row of wheels held by a rod through their centres. The wheels can turn on the rod. Alphabets, in any order, are printed on the wheels' edges. Messages can be enciphered by turning the wheels to set up the plaintext. The plaintext is then enciphered by writing down *any other row of letters* made by the wheels. In this book, only the row ABOVE the plaintext will be used.

You can encipher messages in this way too. Instead of using proper wheels and a rod, make the 'card and can' cipher 'wheels' shown opposite.

Use a clean, smooth, soft-drink can and write the following alphabets on card strips:

STRIP 1	A B C D E F G H I J K L M N O P Q R S T U V W X Y Z
STRIP 2	Z C E G I K M O Q S U W Y B D H F J L N P R X V T A
STRIP 3	D A G J M P S V Y B E H K Q N T W Z C F I X O R U L
STRIP 4	X E I M Q U Y B F T N R V Z C G K O S W D H L P A J
STRIP 5	K F B P U Z A G L Q V C H M R W D I N S X E J T O Y
STRIP 6	S G M A Y B H N T Z C I O D U J P V E K Q W F L R X
STRIP 7	I H O V C A P W B M Q X D K R Y E L S Z F J T G N U
STRIP 8	B I Q Y A J R Z C K S D L T E M U F N V G O W H X P
STRIP 9	T J S C K L B A U G M V N F W D O E X P Y Q H Z I R
STRIP 10	L K U B X V C M W D N A E O Y F P Z G Q H R I S J T

Use your 'wheels' to encipher **MEET ME SOON**. Slide the loops over the can so that the letters make up your plaintext words. Now you can encipher by writing out the row of letters lying **ABOVE** these words. Your cryptogram is **LCBF HV LGDD**.

To decipher your message, your friend must have a can with similar loops around it to set up the cryptogram and read the message from the line **BELOW**.

CARD AND CAN CIPHER 'WHEELS'

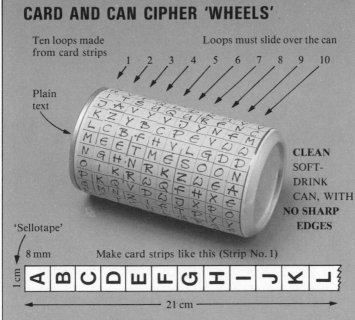

Ten loops made from card strips

Loops must slide over the can

1 2 3 4 5 6 7 8 9 10

Plain text

CLEAN SOFT-DRINK CAN, WITH NO SHARP EDGES

'Sellotape'

8 mm

1 cm

Make card strips like this (Strip No. 1)

| A | B | C | D | E | F | G | H | I | J | K | L |

← 21 cm →

'Sellotape' the ends together to make loops which will slide over the can.

Take the cryptogram from the row above the plaintext –
LCBFHVLGDD

Encipher these following messages, using your wheels – there are some nulls:

RUN QUICKLY   DO NOT MOVE Q
LEAVE KEYS UNDER THE MAT

Now decipher these (again there are some nulls):

TQB FCV VGWA   EGQW JBYE HP
KMZG JBY SDEQ NUXZXY HPP

Note: When messages are longer than 10 letters, carry on from first strip again, putting in breaks and nulls.

41

THE ENIGMA CIPHER MACHINES

Enigma – from the Latin *aenigma*, meaning 'a puzzle' – was a cipher machine (opposite), and thousands of these machines were used by German forces in World War II. British computers deciphered Enigma's cryptograms, revealing Germany's plans and helping to defeat that country in great battles.

The most important thing about Enigma was the electric wiring inside it. This linked the plaintext keyboard to rotors (cipher wheels) and linked those to bulbs which lit up letter windows. You can show how Enigma's rotors turned to give new cipher letters. Use loops 1 and 2 on your card and can 'wheels' (bottom next page).

First set your keyletters on the loops. Use Q C and remember to turn the cipher loop forward (*towards you*) as you encipher each letter. The plaintext is: RUSSIA. To encipher **R** – find **R** on plaintext loop 1. Write its cipher partner on loop 2 (**E**).

TURN CIPHER LOOP 2 ONE LETTER SPACE FORWARD.

To encipher **U** – find **U** on loop 1. Write its cipher partner (**I**).

TURN CIPHER LOOP 2 ONE LETTER SPACE FORWARD.

Carry on for the full cryptogram **E I C Z H M**. To decipher this, you must know the keyletters. Set Q C on the loops. To decipher **E** – find **E** on cipher loop 2. Write its plaintext partner (**R**).

TURN THE CIPHER LOOP ONE LETTER SPACE FORWARD.

To decipher **I** – find **I** on cipher loop 2. Write its plaintext partner (**U**).

TURN THE CIPHER LOOP ONE LETTER SPACE FORWARD.

Carry on for the full plaintext.

THE ENIGMA CIPHER MACHINE

i) Keyletters ① were set up on rotors which lay inside.
ii) Wiring joined plaintext keyboard letters ② to rotors and rotors to bulbs in windows ③.
iii) Plaintext keys were pressed to light up bulbs in windows. Here A has been pressed and enciphered to light up as X.
iv) When letters lit up they were copied down as cryptograms.
v) As each letter lit up, rotors moved one place forward to give new cipher letters.

CARD AND CAN ENIGMA ROTOR

Keyletters

Loop 1 has the plaintext letters.
Do not move it.

Loop 2 has the cipher letters.
Move it one letter space towards you
as you encipher or decipher each letter.

By using your Card and Can rotor, encipher these messages. Set keyletters to A F.

SET THE KEYLETTERS KEEP THIS SECRET

And decipher the following, with the keyletters set to A F once again:

i) NG CCK IUPL   ii) VVJJ UAIZ URSS KJFW

Reset key letters to begin each new cipher.

43

MORSE CODE

Perhaps the most widely used code on Earth is Morse Code. Like many other codes it is *not* secret. Instead it was made up by the American Samuel Finley Breese Morse (1791-1872) to allow messages to be sent quickly along the new electric telegraphs.

Morse built up his code using short dots and long dashes to stand for the letters of the alphabet. The way that this was done was very clever, because Morse decided that he would use only very simple dot and dash code signs for the letters of the alphabet which we use *more than any others* in our words. This would help people to remember and understand his code more easily.

Morse counted the type letters used in a printing office, and found that E was used most often, then came T in second place and in joint third place were A, I, N, O and S. Notice how simply these letters are shown in Morse's dots and dashes, and how easy it is to remember them.

At first Morse found it hard to get people to build telegraphs and use his code. In 1844 however, after building a telegraph line between Baltimore and Washington in the United States, he was able to use it to send his first coded message which was, 'What hath God wrought!'

Morse symbols – Alphabet

A ● ▬	H ● ● ● ●	O ▬ ▬ ▬	V ● ● ● ▬
B ▬ ● ● ●	I ● ●	P ● ▬ ▬ ●	W ● ▬ ▬
C ▬ ● ▬ ●	J ● ▬ ▬ ▬	Q ▬ ▬ ● ▬	X ▬ ● ● ▬
D ▬ ● ●	K ▬ ● ▬	R ● ▬ ●	Y ▬ ● ▬ ▬
E ●	L ● ▬ ● ●	S ● ● ●	Z ▬ ▬ ● ●
F ● ● ▬ ●	M ▬ ▬	T ▬	
G ▬ ▬ ●	N ▬ ●	U ● ● ▬	

Numerals

1 ● ▬ ▬ ▬ ▬		6 ▬ ● ● ● ●
2 ● ● ▬ ▬ ▬		7 ▬ ▬ ● ● ●
3 ● ● ● ▬ ▬		8 ▬ ▬ ▬ ● ●
4 ● ● ● ● ▬		9 ▬ ▬ ▬ ▬ ●
5 ● ● ● ● ●		0 ▬ ▬ ▬ ▬ ▬

Morse code was originally sent by means of sound down a telegraph wire – you can try this method of sending messages by using a buzzer or electric bell.

You can also send Morse code by using a torch. To avoid confusion, make your dash at least three times as long as your dot. Here are some messages for you to decode:

▬ ● ● ● ● ▬ ● ● ▬ ● ▬ ▬ ▬ ▬ ▬ ● ● ▬ ▬ ● ● ● ▬ ● ▬ ● ▬ ▬ ▬ ▬ ● ●
● ▬ ● ● ● ● ● ● ● ● ▬ ▬ ● ● ● ● ● ● ● ▬ ▬ ▬ ● ▬ ▬ ●
● ● ▬ ● ● ▬ ● ▬ ● ● ▬ ● ▬ ● ● ▬ ● ● ▬ ▬ ▬ ● ● ▬ ● ● ● ●
● ● ● ● ▬ ▬ ▬ ● ▬ ● ▬ ▬ ● ● ▬ ▬ ▬ ▬ ● ● ● ● ▬ ▬ ● ▬ ▬
● ▬ ● ● ▬ ▬ ▬ ▬ ● ▬ ▬ ● ▬ ● ● ▬ ● ● ● ● ● ● ● ● ● ●

Now code and send these messages:

DOTS AND DASHES MAKE MORSE MESSAGES
DO NOT MIX UP DOTS AND DASHES

Sometimes people become tramps. They may do this because they are bored by doing the same job day in and day out; they may have lost their job and home through bad luck or they may just seek adventure on the open road. These tramps have their own code and they leave messages for each other by chalking code signs on the gates or walls of houses where they have asked for food or shelter. By doing this, the tramps help each other to make their journeys easier and safer.

The tramps' code was kept secret and was handed down among the tramps over the ages, so it was known only to the tramps themselves. However, about forty years ago, the French police arrested a tramp and by chance, he had a list of code signs and their meanings in his pocket.

A few of these are shown on the next page. Notice how some of the signs give a clear idea of their messages from the way they are drawn. Good examples of this are the jagged 'teeth' line warning of a fierce dog, 'the hot cross bun' sign showing that food may be had and the set of straight 'bars' showing the danger of prison.

Symbol	Meaning	Symbol	Meaning
	Not a good place for tramps		Jagged teeth of fierce dog
	Danger		'Coins' show this house may give money
	Beware of prison		Hot cross bun shows food may be given at this house
	People in authority here		Mouth sign shows householder can be talked into giving the tramps help
	People here offer work. Not good		No good. Many tramps have called at this place already
	Nothing for a tramp here		
	Bad place. People report you to authority		
	Very nasty people here		

47

THE WEATHERMAN'S CODES

99903 772 72720 24615 91212... Did you know that weather forecasts are made from encoded reports like this? Weather stations on land and sea send in such messages at least once every six hours. These stations have to report so many facts so quickly that they need a code to help them to do this.

The code is an International *Meteorological* code (meteorology is the study of weather). It uses groups of figures in a set order. The first and second groups always show the country and station sending the report. The third group always shows facts about cloud and wind − and so on through the groups.

Encoded reports in Britain are sent to the Central Forecasting Office at Bracknell in Berkshire. There they are decoded into plaintext. The plaintext facts are then marked onto maps in special code signs. The maps are filled in to give full weather maps for forecasting.

To understand the figures and the special map signs you will need the Meteorological Office's code book, which is on sale to the public. Opposite you will see what the groups of figures above mean to a weatherman after he has decoded them.

When the weathermen have decoded their reports and filled in their maps, they can make a forecast. On television, they use another set of weather signs to show us their forecasts (see opposite). Notice how simple these have been made to make it easy to understand and remember them.

Figures	Plaintext meanings
	COUNTRY
99903	Great Britain
	WEATHER STATION
772	London Airport
	CLOUD AND WIND
7	$\frac{7}{8}$ Sky clouded over
27	Wind from 270° (West)
20	Wind speed 20 knots
	VIEW AND WEATHER
24	Clear view for 2.4 kilometres
61	Steady rain but not freezing
5	Recent drizzle
	TEMPERATURE AND AIR PRESSURE
912	Air pressure 991.2 millibars
12	Air temperature 12°C

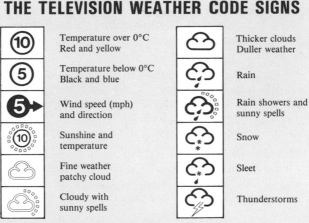

THE TELEVISION WEATHER CODE SIGNS

⑩	Temperature over 0°C Red and yellow	☁	Thicker clouds Duller weather
⑤	Temperature below 0°C Black and blue	☁	Rain
➎►	Wind speed (mph) and direction	☁	Rain showers and sunny spells
⑩	Sunshine and temperature	☁	Snow
☁	Fine weather patchy cloud	☁	Sleet
☁	Cloudy with sunny spells	☁	Thunderstorms

No code sign is used for Fog, which is always in plaintext.

CODES IN MODERN LIFE

Your daily life now runs on codes! The food on your breakfast table has been encoded. A code stamped on milk-bottle tops shows when milk was delivered. Coloured tags on your bread wrappers also show delivery days. Other food may have coded date stamps. These show freshness (eg, 09 09 90 may mean 'Eat before the ninth day of the ninth month in 1990.') When the postman calls, he will bring letters addressed in the postal code.

When walking to school you may use the Green Cross code. If cycling, you must know the meanings of road signs in the Highway Code. If going by car, your driver needs a licence with code numbers on it. Your car also needs plates with code letters and numbers on them.

Go by bus, and your ticket has code numbers on it. Travel by train, and your driver obeys code signs or signals. Your bus and train timetables may have code letters too (eg, 'W' may mean 'Wednesdays only'). The timetables themselves may be worked out by computers which run on coded programmes.

At school, lesson timetables may be encoded (eg, **Eng**lish with Mr **Walker** may be 'Eng Wr'). Papers and exercise books all have code numbers, so that they can be ordered quickly for your use. Look closely at your library books. They will all have code numbers on their spines.

Find out the meanings of these everyday codes – you will then have ideas for making up codes of your own.

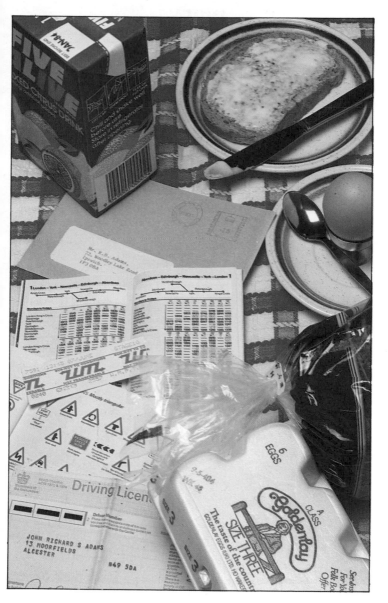

INDEX